This book provided by

raising™
readers

www.raisingreaders.org • Funded by the Libra Foundation

For Nate

First U.S. edition 2016

This edition published specially for Raising Readers 2018 by Candlewick Press

Library of Congress Catalog Card Number 2016943754
ISBN 978-0-7636-8942-1 (Nosy Crow hardcover edition)
ISBN 978-1-5362-0872-6 (Raising Readers edition)

18 WKT 1

Printed in Shenzhen, Guangdong, China

This book was typeset in MillerBanner.
The illustrations were created digitally.

Nosy Crow
an imprint of
Candlewick Press
99 Dover Street
Somerville, Massachusetts 02144

www.nosycrow.com
www.candlewick.com

THERE'S A BEAR ON MY CHAIR

ROSS COLLINS

nosy crow™
An imprint of Candlewick Press

There's a bear
on
my
chair.

He is so big,
it's hard to share.
There isn't any
room to spare.

We do not
make a happy pair,
a mouse and bear
with just one chair.

When I give him
a nasty glare,
he seems completely
unaware.

I don't know
what he's doing there,
that bear who's sitting
on MY chair.

I must admit he has
some flair.
He has fine taste
in leisure wear.
I'm fond of how
he does his hair.

But still I wish he
was not there.

I'll try to tempt him with a pear,
to **lure** him from my favorite chair.

But he just goes on
sitting there.
Why **won't** he
go back
to his lair?

Maybe I'll give him
a scare—

I'll jump out
in my underwear!

But no.
Of course
he does not care.

That stinky bear
sat on my chair.

to:
the BEAR
from:
a friend

That's it! I'm done!
I do declare!
This bear
has led me to
despair!
It is not fair!
It is not fair!
I'm going now.
I don't know where. . . .

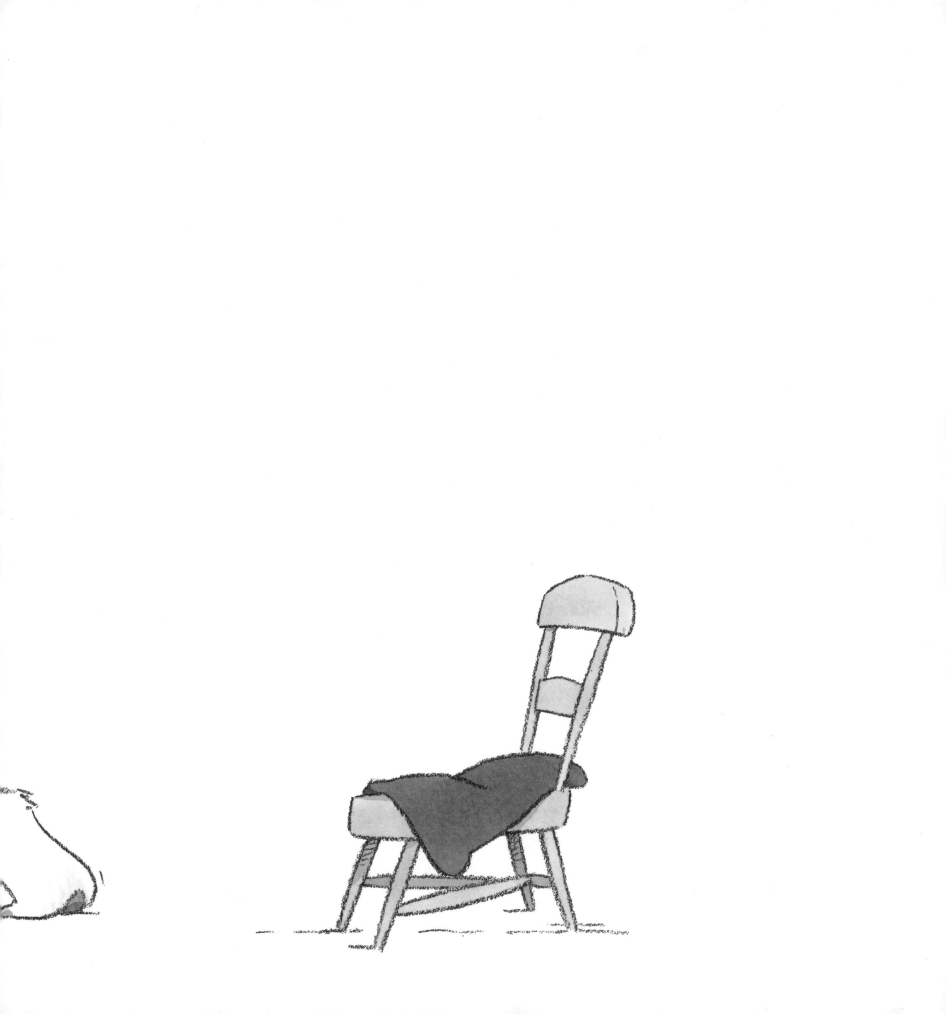

Hey!

There's a mouse
in my house.

10 WAYS TO EXPLORE THIS BOOK

There's a Bear on My Chair

Ross Collins

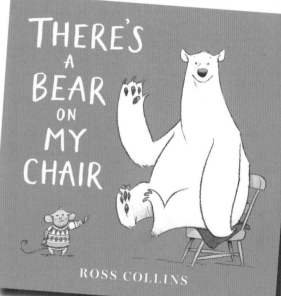

1. **THINK** of all the words that rhyme with *bear*.
2. **MAKE** a small chair for Mouse using things from around your house.
3. **CREATE** a story about Mouse in Bear's house.
4. **TALK** together about ways to get the bear to leave.
5. **LEARN** the meaning of the word *endangered*.
6. **READ** another book about polar bears.
7. **HELP** your child retell the story using the illustrations.
8. **IMITATE** the sounds of a mouse and a bear.
9. **NAME** the mouse and the bear.
10. **COUNT** all the words that appear in red together.

FIVE WAYS TO DISCOVER ANY STORY WITH A CHILD

1. Talk about what the book makes you both think or feel.
2. Sing a song that is related to a character or something in the story.
3. Act out parts of the story.
4. Draw a picture of something that happened in the book.
5. Retell the story using the illustrations.

For more fun activities, check out www.raisingreaders.org.